FRANZ's PHANTASMAGORICAL *MACHINE

Written by
BETH ANDERSON

Illustrated by
CAROLINE HAMEL

Kids Can Press

PHANTASMAGORICAL: having a fantastic or deceptive appearance,
as something in a dream or created by the imagination

For my agent, Stephanie Fretwell-Hill, who believed in this story from the start — B.A.

In loving memory of my father — C.H.

ACKNOWLEDGMENTS

Many thanks to Julie and Ute for German translation, to my steadfast critique partners and to my fantabulous family
for their encouragement. My gratitude also goes to Franz Gsellmann, grandson of the creator of the World Machine;
to Sabine Gruber, manager of the World Machine; and to Dr. James Miller, Edelsbach Tourism Association.

IMAGE CREDITS

Page 11: Permission to illustrate the Atomium, Bruxelles, 1958 © Atomium / SOCAN - 2020 granted by Atomium.
Page 26 & 30: Permission to illustrate the Weltmaschine granted by the estate of Franz Gsellmann.
Page 28: Photo of Franz Gsellmann reproduced with permission of the estate of Franz Gsellmann.
Page 29: Photo of the Weltmaschine reproduced with permission of the estate of Franz Gsellmann.

Published in Canada and the U.S. by Kids Can Press Ltd.
25 Dockside Drive, Toronto, ON M5A 0B5

Kids Can Press is a Corus Entertainment Inc. company

www.kidscanpress.com

The artwork in this book was rendered on a drawing tablet using gouache brushes.
The text is set in Times New Roman.

Edited by Katie Scott and Kathleen Keenan
Designed by Andrew Dupuis

Printed and bound in Shenzhen, China, in 10/2021 by Imago

CM 22 0 9 8 7 6 5 4 3 2 1

LIBRARY AND ARCHIVES CANADA CATALOGUING IN PUBLICATION

Title: Franz's phantasmagorical machine / written by Beth Anderson ; illustrated by Caroline Hamel.
Names: Anderson, Beth, 1954– author. | Hamel, Caroline, illustrator.
Identifiers: Canadiana 20210197234 | ISBN 9781525303258 (hardcover)
Subjects: LCSH: Gsellmann, Franz, 1910–1981 — Juvenile literature. | LCSH: Inventors — Austria — Biography —
Juvenile literature. | LCSH: Machinery — Juvenile literature. | LCGFT: Biographies.
Classification: LCC TJ140.G74 A84 2022 | DDC j621.092—dc23

Kids Can Press gratefully acknowledges that the land on which our office is located is the traditional territory of
many nations, including the Mississaugas of the Credit, the Anishnabeg, the Chippewa, the Haudenosaunee and the
Wendat peoples, and is now home to many diverse First Nations, Inuit and Métis peoples.

We thank the Government of Ontario, through Ontario Creates; the Ontario Arts Council; the Canada Council for
the Arts; and the Government of Canada for supporting our publishing activity.

FSC
www.fsc.org
MIX
Paper from
responsible sources
FSC® C005748

The most beautiful thing we can experience is the mysterious.
It is the source of all true art and science. — Albert Einstein

Franz's eyes twinkled with wonder as the little bird popped out of the cuckoo clock.

He put his ear close to the chirping bird. *What makes the sound?*
He peered at the gears. *What makes them move?*
He peeked behind the small door. *What's going on in there?*

A tiny whisper called him to imagine, discover, create. But his mother had no time for Franz's playing. "Go help your father in the barn."

Each year at school, the whisper grew louder ... with the flutter of pages, the click of the abacus and the scratch of chalk.

Pencil and notebook in hand, Franz envisioned a life of inventing. But his father had no time for Franz's ambitions. "Enough dillydallying."

The farm needed Franz. His schooling was over.

When Franz was grown, he took over the family farm. As he milked cows, slopped hogs and gathered eggs, the whisper continued to call him.

One night while he slept, an idea
lit up his dreams — A FANTASTICAL
MAGICAL
PHANTASMAGORICAL
MACHINE!

Day after day, Franz pondered and paced, sketched and
scrumpled, fussed and fretted. He didn't know where to
start. The machine was unlike anything in all the world.

But his wife had no time for Franz's fantasizing.
"Enough lollygagging."

As Franz opened the newspaper one morning, the whisper rose to a shout. Like the image from his dream, the structure at the world's fair in Belgium was huge, amazing, unique in all the world!

How did they build it? Franz wondered.

Though Franz had never traveled outside Austria before, he packed his bag, rushed to the station and boarded a train for Brussels.

When he arrived at the fair, Franz took in the gleaming structure. He zoomed up its elevator, glided down its escalator and marveled at the colorful lights. Then he sketched each part of the building in his notebook.

Franz dug out his last few coins for a souvenir model — a reminder of how ordinary shapes and lights could become something extraordinary.

Back home, Franz cleared a spare room, covered the windows and locked the door. Then he closed his eyes and listened to his imagination.

The next day, he pedaled to the flea market. There he discovered trinkets and treasures from around the world. Pockets and backpack bulging, he returned home with his haul.

RATTLE
CLATTER
CLANG!

His family jiggled the doorknob. "What's going on in there?"

Franz just smiled. Though he wasn't sure what he was creating, he knew he'd figure it out someday.

Every morning, Franz woke up early to tend to the farm. In the afternoon, he dashed off to his workshop. With pulleys, wheels and lights, his machine grew. And so did the gossip about Franz building a mysterious contraption.

"What's going on in there?" asked the neighbors. They snickered at Franz's lack of skills. But Franz listened only to his imagination.

Week after week, Franz explored the junkyard for just the right parts. Hula-Hoops! Horseshoes! A hair dryer! Wagon heaping, he returned home with his haul.

RATTLE CLATTER CLANG!

With motors, wires and gears, his machine grew. After years of work, Franz had transformed the ordinary into the extraordinary.

"At last!" He tightened the final screw.

One by one, Franz flipped the switches. His grin widened as the machine came to life.

FLASH!

WHOOSH!

DING!

POP...

FIZZLE...

THUNK.

The entire village went dark.

HE DOESN'T KNOW WHAT HE'S DOING.

SILLY FARMER!

THAT MACHINE WILL NEVER WORK.

Word traveled fast — Franz had turned on his mysterious contraption.

"What's going on in there?" Villagers clamored at the windows and barked insults.

Franz said nothing. Though their taunts stung, he refused to give up.

Urged on by the whisper, Franz got back to work. Whistling childhood melodies, he rewired, reworked and reconnected.

Humming Mozart symphonies, he painted, polished and perfected.

After twenty-three years of work, Franz put the last piece in place.

He turned on the machine again. Its hum swelled to a rumble, then to a gentle roar. The floor beneath him vibrated as the behemoth began to whir.

Franz's heart zinged.

Soon, reporters came knocking. "What's going on in there?"

Franz was ready. He let them in.

His stomach tightened as the reporters watched the whirring machine. They scribbled notes … and waited.

"Is it going to do something?" they asked.

Franz's hope fizzled. *The machine* was *doing something. Something amazing.*

Shaking their heads, the reporters shuffled out.

The next day when Franz saw the heart-crushing headline, he fled to the attic.

THE USELESS MIRACLE MACHINE

Doesn't anyone else understand?

As Franz lay there deep in thought, he heard voices outside. He peeked through the window and listened. Did he dare let anyone else in?

But this time, the voices sounded different — excited! He brushed himself off, went downstairs and opened the door. His machine was meant to be shared.

Franz edged his way through the crowd, all the way to the front. There, children peered and pointed and puzzled.

One by one, Franz flipped the fifty-three switches, and the machine awoke.

The children's eyes darted back and forth. Their curious frowns flipped into grins. Giggles erupted.

Spellbound, a little girl whispered, "What's going on in there?"

Franz's face crinkled into a smile as he watched the children's eyes twinkle with wonder. His phantasmagorical machine *did* have a purpose — and finally, Franz had figured it out.

Author's note

Franz's Phantasmagorical Machine is based on the life of Franz Gsellmann (guh-SELL-maan). When I stumbled upon Franz's story, I was fascinated by his creative spirit, imagination and perseverance. He reminded me of myself as a child and of all the kids who love to tinker, build and invent. These days, I use words to build stories. Like Franz's machine, not every story works at first. So I keep fine-tuning the story and hope that in the end it, too, will bring joy and inspiration.

About Franz Gsellmann

Born in 1910 in Edelsbach, Austria, Franz Gsellmann dreamed of being an electrician or a clockmaker. Unfortunately, his education was interrupted by World War I, illness and farmwork. At age fourteen, after completing the fourth grade, he left school to work on the family farm.

Franz had a calling to build and invent, and he tinkered for many years. One morning, he awoke from a dream with a vision of a machine, but he had no idea where to start. At age 48, Franz found the inspiration he needed at the 1958 World's Fair in Brussels, Belgium. There he saw the Atomium, a 102 m (335 ft.) building with nine giant spheres representing iron atoms (the small building blocks for all matter). When Franz returned home, he got started on his machine.

Though his education was limited, Franz's imagination and enthusiasm were not. He assembled treasures from flea markets and junkyards without knowing the end result. Over 23 years, his machine grew to 6 m (20 ft.) long, 3 m (10 ft.) high and 2 m (7 ft.) wide. Shortly before his death in 1981, Franz finally completed his creation. He hoped that one day it would benefit others in some way.

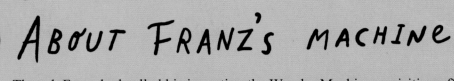

About Franz's Machine

Though Franz had called his invention the Wonder Machine, a visiting official named it the World Machine (*Weltmaschine* in German). The new name was a good fit: the machine had parts from around the world and a connection to a world's fair.

The World Machine is an example of outsider art, a kind of art made by self-taught artists that shows thinking outside the box. Like many artists, Franz saw beauty, potential and meaning where others didn't. Like many scientists, he was inspired by questions and embarked on an experimental journey. His machine is an interesting example of the intersection between art and science.

Franz's machine encouraged other artists to explore mechanical-kinetic sculptures (machine-like art that moves). His story is a reminder that many of us have an urge to create and ideas to share. Even though some people may laugh at these creations or ideas, it's often outsiders like Franz who show us new ways to think about the world.

Share Your Ideas!

What makes a machine useful?
Is make-it-up-as-you-go a good strategy? Why or why not?
What was the purpose and significance of Franz's machine?

THE WORLD MACHINE

Franz's machine contained more than 1,960 parts — more than can be listed here. How many of these items can you find on this page?

10 fans

9 bells

8 whistles

7 springs

6 flower lights

5 lampshades

4 faucets

3 switches

2 magnets

1 photo of Franz Gsellmann

See the answer key on the next page!

BOOKS ABOUT OTHER CREATORS

Aronson, Sarah and Robert Neubecker. *Just Like Rube Goldberg: The Incredible True Story of the Man Behind the Machines.* New York: Beach Lane Books, 2019.

Aston, Dianna Hutts **and** Susan L. Roth. *Dream Something Big: The Story of the Watts Towers.* New York: Dial Books, 2011.

Davis, Kathryn Gibbs **and** Gilbert Ford. *Mr. Ferris and His Wheel.* Boston: HMH Books for Young Readers, 2014.

Tate, Don and R. Gregory Christie. *It Jes' Happened: When Bill Traylor Started to Draw.* New York: Lee & Low Books, 2012.

AUTHOR'S SOURCES

WEBSITES

Gsellmann Weltmaschine
www.weltmaschine.at

BOOKS

Roth, Gerhard. "Franz Gsellmann: Die Weltmaschine Am Ende Der Welt [The World Machine at the End of the World]." Chapter 8 in *Portraits*. Frankfurt: S. Fischer Verlag, 2012.

ARTICLES

Koffler, Sandy, ed. "The Atomium: Focal Point for Millions of Visitors." UNESCO Courier 10, no. 7 (1957): 6–7. https://unesdoc.unesco.org/ark:/48223/pf0000078347.

Stürmer, Ariane. "Absurdes Kunstwerk: Die wundersame Weltmaschine [Absurd Artwork: The Wondrous World Machine]." Spiegel Online (Hamburg). November 11, 2008. https://www.spiegel.de/geschichte/absurdes-kunstwerk-a-948007.html.

ANSWER KEY

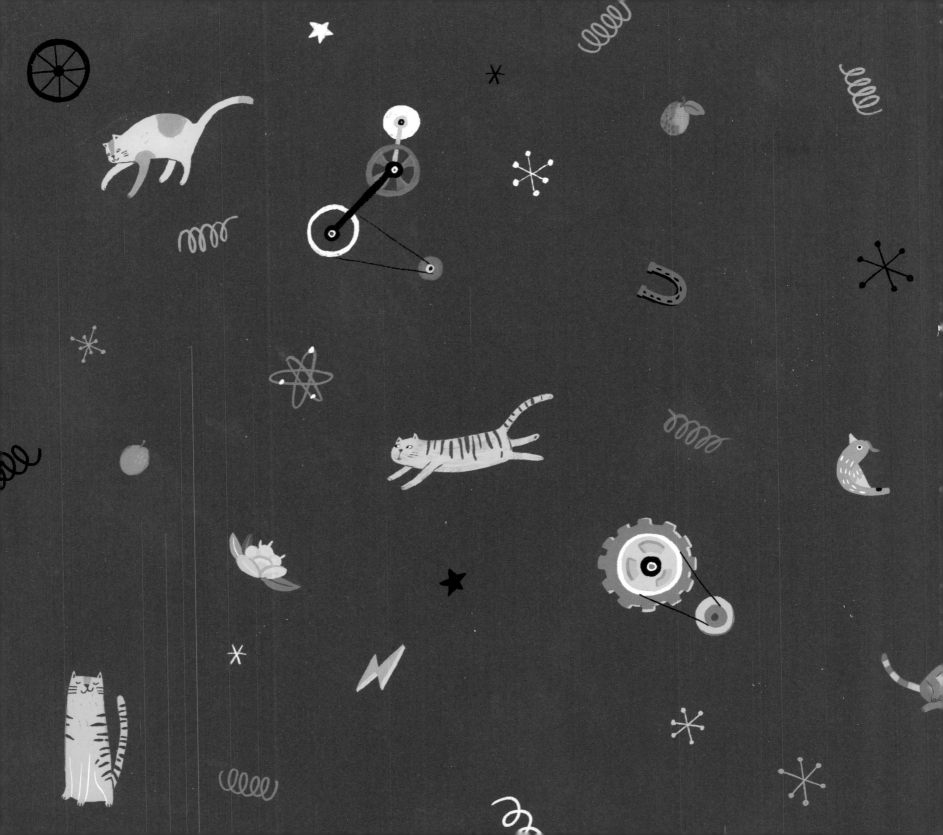